THE FOUR MUSICIANS

by

Jakob and Wilhelm Grimm

Illustrated by Tony Palazzo

Once upon a time there were four runaways who decided to go to Bremen to become the town musicians. They were a donkey, a dog, a cat and a cock, and little did they know when they set out for town what adventures awaited them in the forest. This is a favorite tale for children, told and retold for over a hundred years.

* *

Classification and Dewey Decimal: Folklore (398.2)

About the Authors:

JAKOB AND WILHELM GRIMM spent thirteen years collecting their folk tales, always directly from the lips of the people and never embroidering the truth. These tales were written to interest people of all ages. Both brothers were students of philology (the study of language) and law. They worked as librarians and as teachers at many universities in Germany. Their folk tales have been published in most languages and have been read and loved by many generations.

About the Illustrator:

Illustrating children's books was a hobby with TONY PALAZZO when he worked as art director for advertising agencies and a national magazine. It is now a full-time job. He has exhibited his paintings in a number of galleries in New York and many other parts of the country. He and his wife live in Hastings-on-Hudson, New York.

The FOUR

MUSICIANS

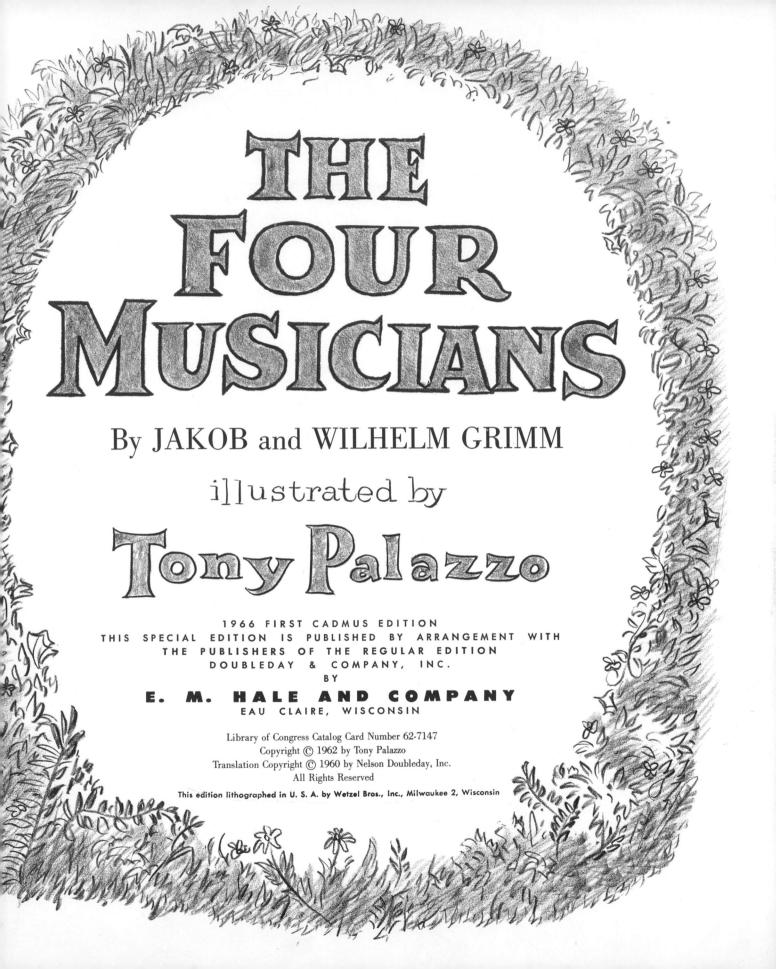

THE FOUR MUSICIANS

By JAKOB and WILHELM GRIMM

illustrated by

Tony Palazzo

1966 FIRST CADMUS EDITION
THIS SPECIAL EDITION IS PUBLISHED BY ARRANGEMENT WITH
THE PUBLISHERS OF THE REGULAR EDITION
DOUBLEDAY & COMPANY, INC.
BY

E. M. HALE AND COMPANY
EAU CLAIRE, WISCONSIN

Library of Congress Catalog Card Number 62-7147
Copyright © 1962 by Tony Palazzo
Translation Copyright © 1960 by Nelson Doubleday, Inc.

Near the town of Bremen lived a man who owned a donkey. The poor beast had worked hard all his life, but at last grew old and unfit for his work. Therefore, his master decided to sell him to the tanner. The donkey, however, sensed what was in the wind and ran away. Taking the road to Bremen, he trotted along until he found a dog by the wayside, who was panting as if he had run for his life.

"Why are you panting so?" asked the donkey.

"Oh!" said the dog, "I ran away from my master. He wants to kill me because I am getting old and weak. But what am I to do now?"

"I'll tell you," said the donkey. "I am going to Bremen to become a town musician. Come with me, and while I play the lute you can beat the drum."

The dog liked the idea very much, and they traveled on together.
Soon afterward they came upon a cat who looked as gloomy as three
rainy days.

"Why are you so unhappy?" asked the donkey.

"Meow," complained the cat, "who would be gay when his life is in danger? Now that I am too old to hunt mice, my mistress wants to drown me. So I have run off. But what shall I do now?"

"Come with us to Bremen," said the donkey. "You are a wonderful serenader; you can become a town musician too."

The cat was very pleased and went with them.

Soon the three runaways passed by a farmhouse where a cock, perched on a gate, was crowing as loud as he could.

"Your crowing shatters my eardrums!" cried the donkey. "What is wrong with you?"

"This very morning, as I prophesied good weather," answered the cock, "out came our mistress and told the cook that I must be made into soup. Tonight I am to have my head cut off, so I want to crow now, just as long as I can."

"Dear Chanticleer," said the donkey, "you had much better come with us. We are going to Bremen. With your fine singing voice, we will make a wonderful quartet."

The cock agreed, and all four went on together. But they could not reach Bremen in one day.

As night came on, they passed through a wood where they decided to rest. Before they went to sleep, however, the cock flew up to the top of a tall tree and looked all around. In the distance he saw a little light shining, so he told his companions that there must be a house not far off. They all decided to go in the direction of the light.

As they came nearer the light grew brighter, and soon they came upon a robbers' house.

The donkey, being the biggest, went up to the window and looked in. There he saw a table covered with fine food and drink; and the robbers were sitting around it enjoying themselves.

As the four companions were very hungry, they held a council to decide how they could best drive the robbers out; and finally they agreed on a good plan.

They crept to the window, where the donkey placed his forefeet on the window sill. The dog climbed on the donkey's back, and the cat on the dog's, and the cock flew up and perched on the cat's head.

At a given signal
the donkey started to bray,

the dog to bark,

the cat to mew,

and the cock to crow.

At this dreadful noise the robbers jumped up, thinking that
nothing less than an ogre had come in, and—scared to death—they
ran away into the wood. The four musicians then sat down at
the table and ate their fill. When they were finished,
they put out the lights, and each one looked for a
comfortable sleeping place.

The donkey went to sleep on a pile of straw in the yard, the dog behind the door, the cat on the hearth, and the cock settled himself on the rooftop.

And as they all were very tired from their journey,
they soon fell fast asleep.

After midnight, since all was very quiet, one of the robbers came back to search the house. He went into the kitchen to light a candle, and thinking that the cat's shining eyes were live coals, he held a match to them to light it.

But the cat, who wouldn't put up with such nonsense, flew into his face, spitting and scratching. Dreadfully frightened, the robber tried to run away, stumbling toward the back door.

The dog, who was lying there, jumped up and bit his leg.

As the man dashed through the yard, the donkey gave him a painful kick with his hind foot.

Then the cock, who had been awakened by the noise, cried out: "Cock-a-doodle-doo!"

The man ran back to the robber captain as hard as he could, shouting: "Oh! In that house is a gruesome witch who scratched me with her long nails; and by the door stands a man with a knife who stabbed me in the leg; and in the yard is a black monster who beat me with a wooden club; and up on the roof there sits a judge who cried: 'Bring the scoundrel up here!' And so I escaped as fast as I could."

From then on the robbers never ventured into the house again. But the four musicians liked it so well that they decided not to go on to Bremen after all. And if they still live, you may find them in a little house in the wood on the road to Bremen.

The FOUR

MUSICIANS